D0646685

Isabella
Girl in Charge

JUST HOW BIG CAN A LITTLE GIRL DREAM?

story by Jennifer Fosberry • pictures by Mike Litwin

sourcebooks
jabberwocky

For Cynthia, who taught me to take charge.

– JF

For Nana, who was always in charge.

– ML

Sourcebooks and the colophon are registered trademarks of Sourcebooks, Inc.

Art was sketched with blueline pencil and rendered in Adobe Photoshop CC.

Published by Sourcebooks Jabberwocky, an imprint of Sourcebooks, Inc.
P.O. Box 4410, Naperville, Illinois 60567-4410
(630) 961-3900
Fax: (630) 961-2168
www.sourcebooks.com

Library of Congress Cataloging-in-Publication data is on file with the publisher.

Source of Production: Phoenix Color, Hagerstown, Maryland, USA
Date of Production: August 2016
Run Number: 5007182

Printed and bound in the United States of America.
PHC 10 9 8 7 6 5 4 3 2 1

"I'm ready," said the little girl.
"Let's go!"

"It's not time, Isabella," the mother said.
"It's not even daylight."

"My name is not Isabella,"
said the little girl.

"I am **SUSANNA**, mayor of this here town."

"Well, Susanna, a little more sleep, please. I don't think we're in **KANSAS** anymore."

"I'm ready," said the little girl. "Let's go!"

"It's not time, Susanna," the mother said. "Breakfast first."

"*My name is not Susanna*," said the little girl.

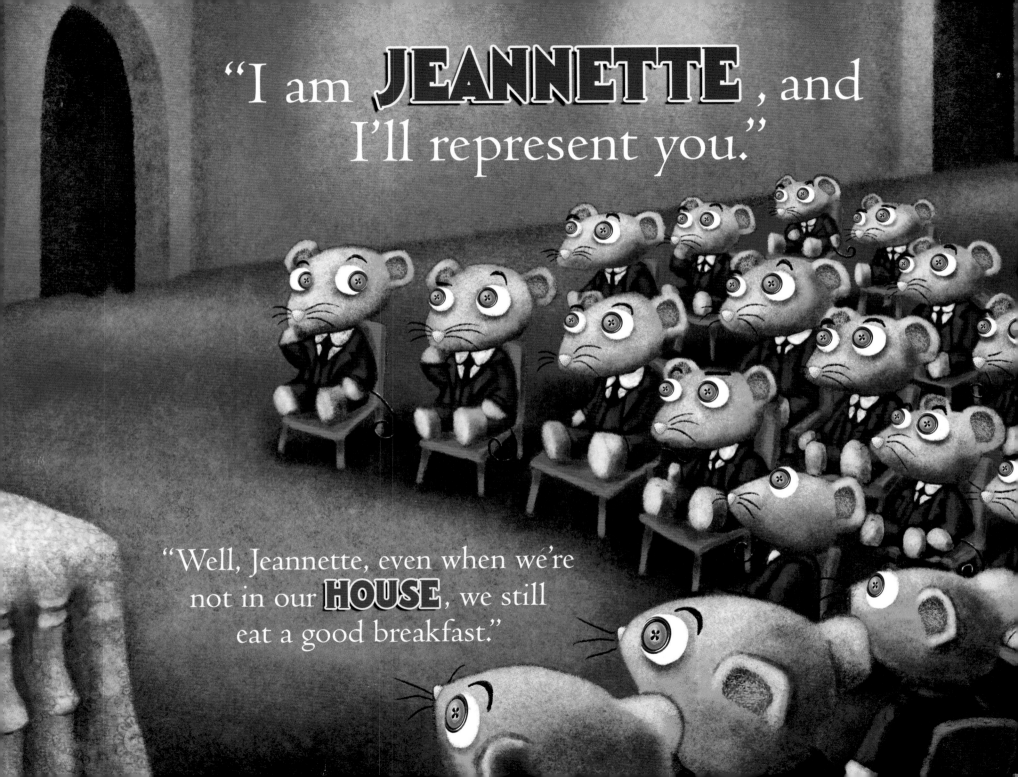

"Let's VOTE on breakfast. I want doughnuts," said the little girl.

"Your father and I vote oatmeal. That's two to one for a healthy breakfast."

"That's not fair," said the little girl.

"We each get one vote. That's FAIR, Jeannette," said the father.

"My name is not Jeannette," said the little girl.

"I'm ready," said the little girl.
"Let's go!"

"It's not time, Nellie,"
the mother said.

"My name is not Nellie," said the little girl.

"I am **FRANCES.**
New Deal—let's go."

"Well, Frances, we need to
check out first. Please pack
your things from the
CABINET."

"I will help with that at a **MINIMUM.**"

"I'm ready," said the little girl. "Let's go!"
"It's not time, Frances," the mother said.

"My name is not Frances," said the little girl.

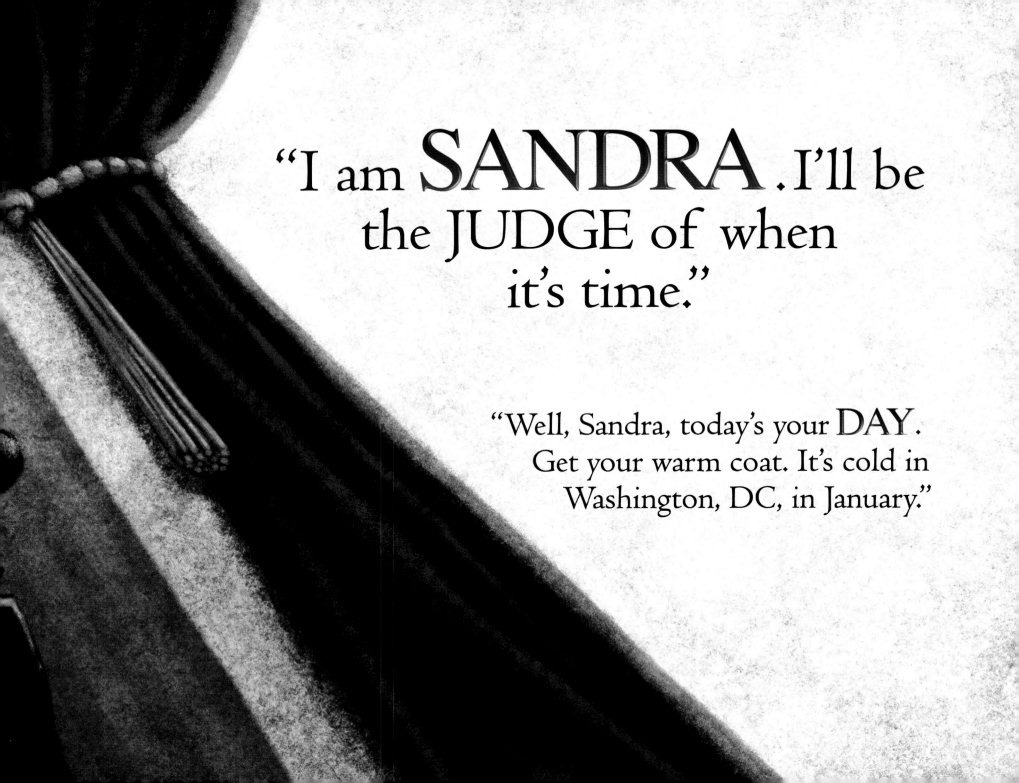

"I am SANDRA. I'll be the JUDGE of when it's time."

"Well, Sandra, today's your DAY. Get your warm coat. It's cold in Washington, DC, in January."

"Is it time?" asked the little girl.
"It's time!" the mother said.

"Let's hurry," the little girl said.

"**CAPITAL** idea!" said the father.

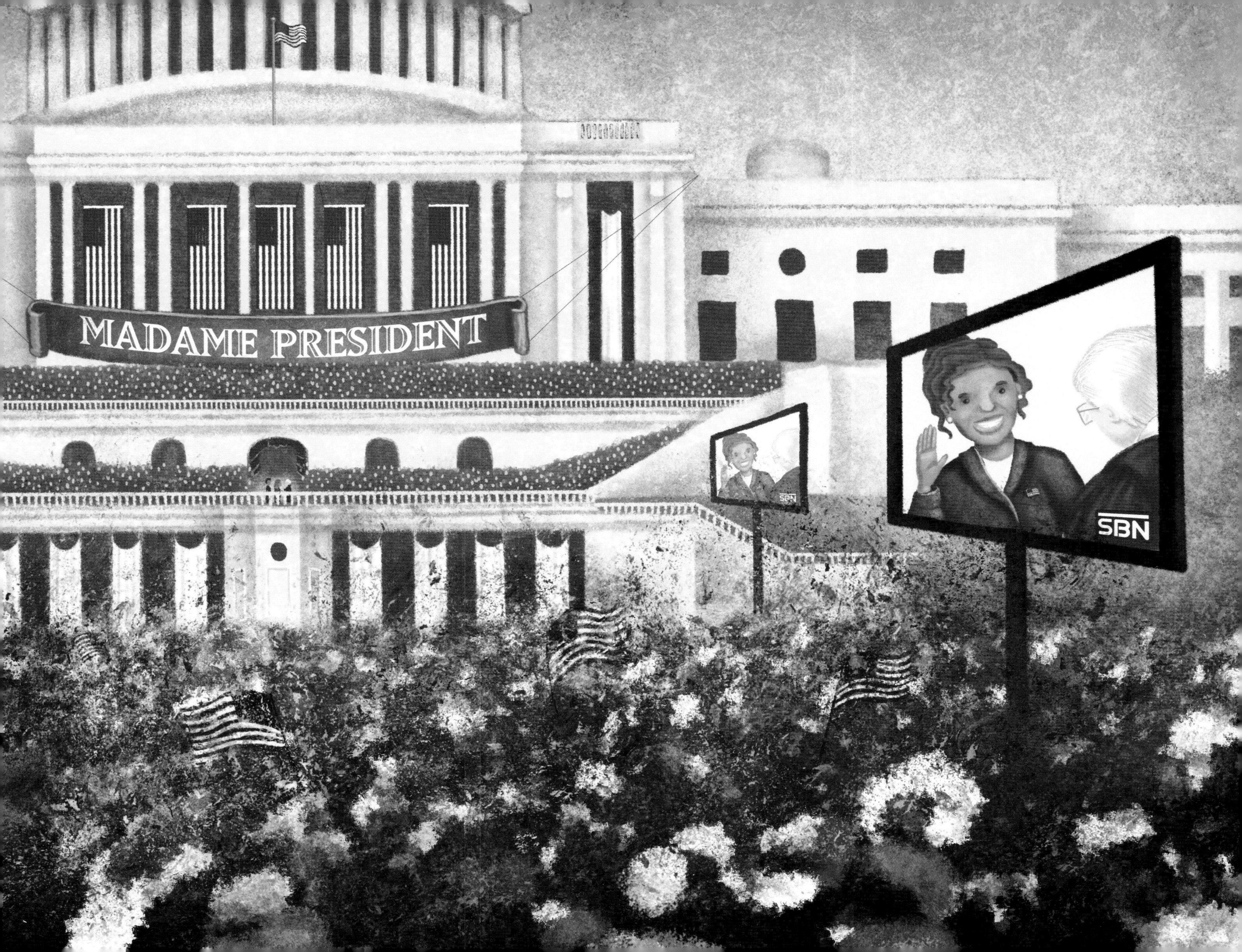
MADAME PRESIDENT
SBN
SBN

it's time!

A timeline of women in U.S. politics

> " Why not nominate women for important places? [...] We shall never have equal rights until we take them, nor respect until we command it. "
>
> —BELVA LOCKWOOD,
> second woman to seek the presidency

Susanna Madora Salter
(1860–1961), first woman mayor

Born in Ohio, Susanna's family soon moved to Kansas. In college, she met Lewis Salter, son of the former Kansas Lt. Governor. They married and settled in Argonia. Susanna's father was elected mayor, while her husband was the city clerk. Kansas gave women the right to vote in 1887. A local Women's Temperance group became involved in politics. Some men thought women should not be involved. On election day, these men put Mrs. Salter on the ballot for mayor. It was a joke, meant to teach the women a lesson. Susanna said she would serve if elected. The Republican Party campaigned for her and she won, becoming the first female mayor in the United States. She served one year in the role, running city meetings with a professional manner.

1860s

1869: First "state" to allow women to vote, Wyoming Territory, preserved in statehood

1870s

1872: First woman to run for president, Victoria Woodhull

1880s

1887: First woman mayor, Susanna Salter, Argonia, Kansas

"*When people keep telling you that you can't do a thing, you kind of like to try it.*"

—MARGARET CHASE SMITH,
Republican Senator, Maine, first woman to serve in the House and Senate, first woman named a nominee for president in major party convention, 1964

Nellie Tayloe Ross

(1876–1977), first woman governor

Nellie was born in Missouri and taught kindergarten in Nebraska when her family moved there. While visiting relatives in Tennessee, she met and married the lawyer William Ross. They moved to Wyoming and later he was elected governor. Nellie was involved with the Cheyenne Women's Club and dedicated to the Temperance movement, advocating for Prohibition. William died in office and Nellie was elected to replace him, becoming the first woman governor. She was not re-elected, but stayed involved with the Democratic Party. Franklin Delano Roosevelt named her Director of the Federal Mint, the first woman to hold that position.

Jeannette Rankin

(1880–1973), first woman elected to Congress

Jeannette was the eldest of six children, whom she helped raise. She studied biology at the University of Montana. Declining several marriage proposals because she feared losing her freedom, she worked as a teacher. After successfully working to get women the vote in Montana, she ran for the U.S. House of Representatives. In 1917, she beat seven men, becoming the first woman in Congress (although there were no women's bathrooms at the time). While in the House, she proudly introduced the legislation that became the Nineteenth Amendment to the U.S. Constitution, giving women the right to vote. Perhaps she is most noted as the only person to vote against entering World War I (sixth day in office) and against entering World War II (in her second term twenty-two years later). She remained dedicated to idea of world peace for her entire life.

"*If I am remembered for no other act, I want to be remembered as the only woman who ever voted to give women the right to vote.*"

—JEANNETTE RANKIN

1890s	1910s	1920s
1894: First women elected to State Legislature, Clara Cressingham, Carrie Holly, and Frances Klock, Colorado	**1916**: First woman elected to the House of Representatives, Jeannette Rankin, Montana	**1920**: Nineteenth Amendment ratified, women get the vote **1922**: First woman to serve in the Senate, Rebecca Latimer Felton, Georgia **1925**: First woman elected Governor, Nellie Tayloe Ross, Wyoming

> *The door might not be opened to a woman again for a long, long time, and I had a kind of duty to other women to walk in and sit down on the chair that was offered, and so establish the right of others long hence and far distant in geography to sit in high seats.*
>
> —FRANCES PERKINS

Frances Perkins

(1880–1965), first woman Cabinet member, Secretary of Labor

Madame Secretary was born in Boston and graduated from Mt. Holyoke when most women did not attend college. She studied the dangerous working conditions in local factories. Later, while working in New York City, she saw women jump to their death from the eight floor during the tragic Triangle Shirtwaist Factory fire. Only one elevator worked and the poor, immigrant workers had no other way to escape. Frances worked to improve working conditions. Governor Al Smith appointed her to the New York Industrial Commission in 1919; she continued in this post for Governor Franklin Delano Roosevelt. When FDR was elected president in 1932, he asked Frances to serve as Secretary of Labor. Worried about her teenage daughter and ill husband, she thought of declining. Convinced of how much good she could do, she accepted, becoming the first woman to serve on the Cabinet and be in line of succession to the presidency. FDR served for four terms and every term Frances resigned and reaccepted the position. Her work led to the Wagner-Peyser Act (which created jobs for millions), minimum wage, maximum work hours, social security and an end to child labor.

1930s

1931: First woman elected to U.S. Senate, Hattie Wyatt Caraway, Arkansas

1933: First woman appointed to Cabinet, Frances Perkins, Secretary of Labor

1960s

1964: First Asian-American woman elected to Congress, Patsy Matsu Takemoto Mink, Hawaii; First woman named nominee for president, Margaret Chase Smith

1966: First African-American woman federal judge, Constance Baker Motley

1968: First African-American woman elected to House of Representatives, Shirley Chisholm, New York; First African-American woman nominated for president, Charlene Mitchell, Communist Party

1970s

1970: First Jewish woman elected to Congress, Bella Abzug, New York

1972: First Asian-American woman runs for President, Patsy Matsu Takemoto Mink

1975: First woman elected governor (not succeeding husband), Ella Grasso, Connecticut

1977: First African-American woman appointed to the Cabinet, two different positions on the Cabinet, Patricia Roberts Harris, Secretary of U.S. Department of Housing and Urban Development, Health & Human Services

Sandra Day O'Connor
(1930—), first woman appointed to the Supreme Court

Sandra grew up part-time on the Lazy B Ranch in Arizona and spent the school year in El Paso, Texas with her grandmother. At the age of 16 she started college. In 1952 she graduated from Stanford Law School. Even with her degree, she was offered work as a secretary, as most lawyers were men at the time. Her first job was as a Deputy County Attorney for San Mateo, California. She raised three sons before continuing her career. Elected to the Arizona State Senate, in three years she was the State Majority Leader, the first woman in the U.S. to hold that role. Elected Judge, she rose to the Arizona Court of Appeals. In 1981 President Ronald Reagan nominated her to the U.S. Supreme Court, and members of the Senate confirmed her unanimously. During her time on the court, she was the swing vote on many important, critical cases before retiring in 2006.

1980s

1981: First woman appointed to the U.S. Supreme Court, Sandra Day O'Connor

1984: First woman to run for vice president on a major party presidential ticket, Geraldine Ferraro

1989: First Cuban American and Latina woman in Congress, Ileana Ros-Lehtinen, Florida

1990s

1993: First woman Attorney General, Janet Reno

1993: First African-American woman elected to the U.S. Senate, Carol Moseley Braun, Illinois

1997: First woman Secretary of State, Madeleine Albright

2000s

2005: First African-American woman National Security Advisor, Condoleezza Rice

2009: First Latina woman appointed to U.S. Supreme Court, Sonia Sotomayor

list of works consulted

If you are interested in these girls or other girls in charge, try some of the following:

BOOKS:

Thimmesh, Catherine. *Madam President the Extraordinary, True (and Evolving) Story of Women in Politics.* Illustrated by Douglas B. Jones. Boston: Houghton Mifflin Co., 2004.

Kimmel, Elizabeth Cody. *Ladies First: 40 Daring American Women Who Were Second to None.* Washington, DC: National Geographic, 2006.

Krull, Kathleen. *Lives of Extraordinary Women, Rulers, and Rebels and What the Neighbors Thought.* San Diego: Harcourt, 2000.

WEBSITES:

Kansas Historical Society. "Susanna Madora Salter." Kansapedia. Last modified March 2016. https://www.kshs.org/kansapedia/susanna-madora-salter/12191.

Rea, Tom. "The Ambition of Nellie Tayloe Ross." WyoHistory. http://www.wyohistory.org/essays/ambition-nellie-tayloe-ross.